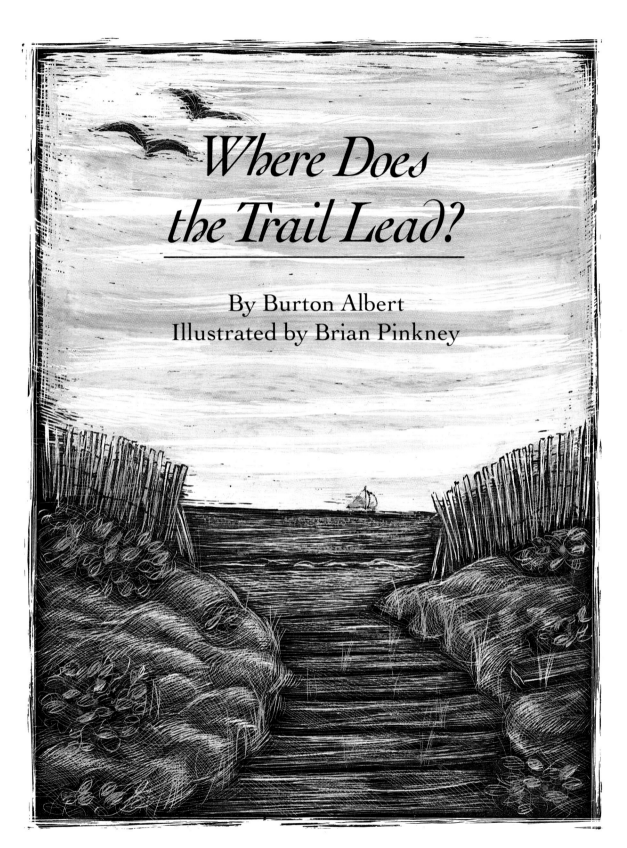

Where Does the Trail Lead?

By Burton Albert
Illustrated by Brian Pinkney

Simon & Schuster Books for Young Readers

PUBLISHED BY SIMON & SCHUSTER
NEW YORK · LONDON · TORONTO · SYDNEY · TOKYO · SINGAPORE

SIMON & SCHUSTER BOOKS FOR YOUNG READERS
Simon & Schuster Building, Rockefeller Center
1230 Avenue of the Americas, New York, New York 10020
Text copyright © 1991 by Burton Albert
Illustrations copyright © 1991 by Brian Pinkney
All rights reserved including the right
of reproduction in whole or in part in any form.
SIMON & SCHUSTER BOOKS FOR YOUNG READERS
is a trademark of Simon & Schuster.

The text was set in 18 point Cochin.
The illustrations were prepared as
scratchboard renderings, handcolored with oil pastels.

Designed by Sylvia Frezzolini.
Manufactured in the United States of America

10 9 8 7 6 5 4 3 2 1
(pbk) 10 9 8 7 6 5 4 3 2 1

Library of Congress Cataloging-in-Publication Data
Albert, Burton.   Where does the trail lead? / by Burton Albert ;
illustrated by Brian Pinkney.   Summary: With the smell of the sea
always in his nostrils, a boy follows an island path through flowers
and pine needles, over the dunes, to a reunion with his family
at the edge of the sea.   [1. Seashore—Fiction.]
I. Pinkney, Brian. ill.   II. Title.
PZ7.A318Wh   1991   90-21450
[E]—dc20   CIP   AC
ISBN: 0-671-73409-1   ISBN: 0-671-79617-8 (pbk)

To Lois and the
lures of Nantucket
B.A.

To my sister, Troy
and my brothers, Scott and Myles
B.P.

On Summertime Island,
where does the trail lead?
Over hills and hollows
of buttercups and snapdragons…

...to a lighthouse at the edge of the sea.

Where does the trail lead?
Past tree limbs bent by the wind,
and tide-pools of periwinkles...

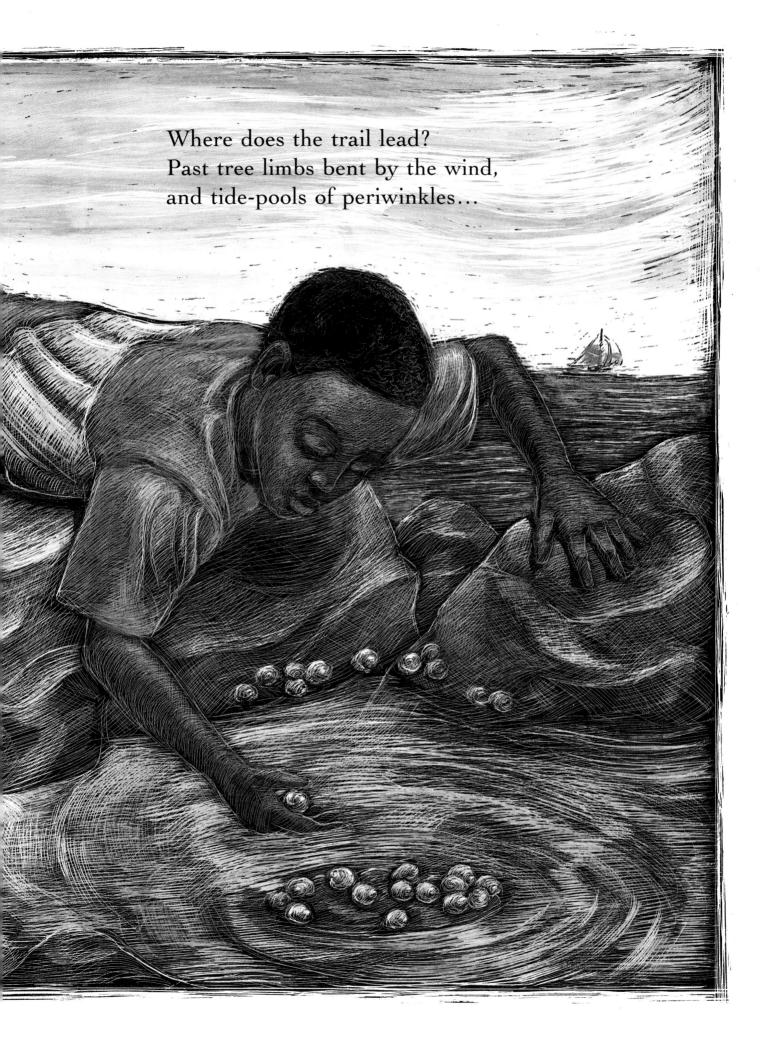

...to gulls in flight at the edge of the sea.

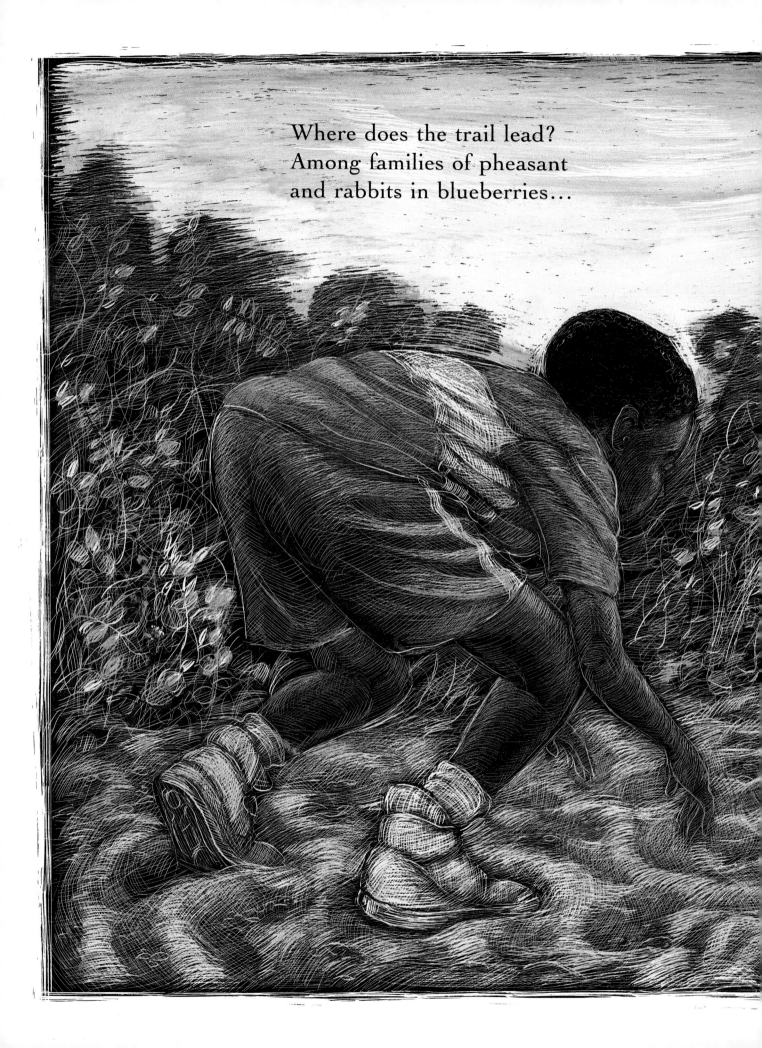

Where does the trail lead?
Among families of pheasant
and rabbits in blueberries...

...to a crest of dunes
at the edge of the sea.

On Summertime Island
where does the trail lead?
Beside old tracks, grown over with grass,
where a rickety train once ran...

...to a ghost town of shanties at the edge of the sea.

Where does the trail lead?
Over the crunch of pine needles—dried and brown.
Beneath the V's and honks of geese…

...to a boat's bow of cattails at the edge of the sea.

Where does the trail lead?
Down a zig-zag of ruts from trucks in the sand.
Along railings of fence on a rocky rim…

...to the roar of surfers' waves
at the edge of the sea.

On Summertime Island,
where does the trail lead?
Back to the crackle of campfires
and the smell of fresh-caught fish…

...to the shimmerings
and shadows of a sinking sun

in the twilight at the edge of the sea.